THE
SILENT
TAKE OVER

BY
PETER "WOLFIE" WOLFINGER

THE SILENT TAKE OVER

1210 SW 23rd PL • Ocala, FL 34471 • Phone 352-622-1825
Website: www.atlantic-pub.com • Email: sales@atlantic-pub.com
SAN Number: 268-1250

Library of Congress Control Number: 2023923406

Printed in the United States

Front cover image is AI-generated.

PROJECT MANAGER: Crystal Edwards
INTERIOR LAYOUT AND JACKET DESIGN: Nicole Sturk

TABLE OF CONTENTS

ACKNOWLEDGMENTS vii

PROLOGUE 1

ONE MONTH LATER. 5

THE FOLLOWING DAY 7

SCHOOL. 11

SWIM MEET 15

GRADUATION PICTURE 19

PROM DAY 21

PROM NIGHT 25

RECRUITING STATION. 31

GRADUATION DAY 33

BOOT CAMP. 37

NEW YEAR'S EVE. 41

LOG CABIN. 47

COLLEGE. 49

EL PASO ARMY BASE 59

MEXICO 61

EL PASO CAMP 65

THE LAST MISSION 69

MEETING 71

RESCUE 73

THREE WEEKS LATER 77

THE WEDDING 81

6 YEARS LATER 85

HOLIDAYS .97

MEDIA NEWS 99

JANUARY 10 101

ONE YEAR LATER 103

THE POWER OF THE MEDIA 105

THE PRICE OF FREEDOM

AMERICAN REVOLUTION
(1775-1783)
4,435 CASUALTIES

WAR OF 1812
(1812-1815)
2,260 CASUALTIES

WORLD WAR I
(1917-1918)
116,516 CASUALTIES

WORLD WAR II
(1941-1945)
405,399 CASUALTIES

KOREAN WAR
(1950-1953)
36,574 CASUALTIES

VIETNAM WAR
(1964-1975)
58,220 CASUALTIES

DESERT SHIELD/DESERT STORM
(1990-1991)
383 CASUALTIES

ENDURING FREEDOM/IRAQI FREEDOM
(OCT 2001- 2014)
3,481 CASUALTIES

ACKNOWLEDGMENTS

While this is my fourth book, my acknowledgments will always be the same. While not a religious person, I do believe in God and angels, and it's because of them I have lived this long.

I would like to thank our Lord for allowing me to live long enough to write this story. I'm sure that when I go home, He will give me a bill for a chiropractor for the many times He carried me throughout my life.

Many thanks to my wife and my friends for their support. And to "Alexa for all the times I have asked her to spell a word.

Another special thanks to Crystal Edwards and her team at Atlantic Publishing Group. They believed in my manuscript and helped this dream come true.

Last but not least, thanks to life. We do not realize how precious life is until we are about to lose it.

PROLOGUE

The year was 1966. The U.S. was in Vietnam as the war escalated and could not get enough supplies to shore by ship to support the military and turned to China for help.

It was a hot night in Saigon when the CIA and Chinese agents met in the hotel. After polite small talk, they got right to the pressing subject: loading piers.

After a long evening of negotiation, a deal was made. For $1 million, China would build the loading piers, and at the end of the war, China will be allowed to enter the fair-trade business as Japan had done.

The deal was made, and it was the beginning of America's downfall.

In 1979, China reformed, making it one of the fastest growing economies in the world.

The year was 2010, China's leader sat with his two sons, both of whom were genetically enhanced. The oldest son, Elwin Wong, age

21, was 6 feet tall. He had black hair and hazel eyes, weighed about 198 pounds, and had an IQ of 165. Even though his mother was American, his Chinese traits were evident. He is fluent in Spanish, Chinese, and English. He also had a black belt in kung fu.

His younger brother, Peter Walker, was 17 and had an IQ of 160. His mother was the sister of Elwin's mother. Peter was born with all the characteristics and traits of white males, with blond hair and blue eyes, and he was extremely handsome. By the time he was 17, he spoke English, Chinese, and Spanish, held a black belt in karate, stood 6-foot two-inches, and weighed 210 pounds of pure muscle.

Elwin and Peter's father spoke in a stern yet soft voice as he explained to them that they were the key to taking over America without a fight.

"I believe we can make America like Hong Kong. This is very important because our population is rising while our arable land is declining. 80 percent of our people live on 20 percent of our land. America has the most arable land in the world. We need their land and resources, which is enough for both countries. But we cannot afford a war as it would destroy the land we need. If we use ground forces, there would be a rifle behind every blade of grass. This is why we have to take our time.

"It will take about 20 or so more years, but this plan has been in effect since 1966 and it's getting close to completion. The first task is for Elwin to go to America and take over the corporation that China holds. The goal is to buy all media companies and put puppet CEOs in charge of the companies. And Peter, you will enter politics when the time is right.

"In recent years, we have been able to smuggle in our citizens. They are male Christians working a trade—electrician, plumber, carpenter, air conditioning, laborers, tech. They all speak English and have been instructed to mingle with the population and marry Chinese or Spanish. For years they have been coming over the border with the Mexicans. And we are close to making up 40 percent of the U.S. population.

"Both of you have American birth certificates and social security cards. Elwin, you were born in New York, and your mother died in childbirth. As far as you know, your mother was American and your father was a Chinese merchant. Your father was much older than your mother, and he passed away from lung cancer. Peter you were also born in New York, and your father and mother were killed in a car accident. Your mother told you of your cousin, Elwin, and told you to seek him out should anything happen to her, that is how you came to live with him. Elwin will say that both sisters were left money, leaving you both financially well. Everything be well documented to back up your stories.

"Now comes the hard part. Both of you will have reversable vasectomies to make sure you do not make a mistake. I will be sending along a young woman named Tiffany, who has volunteered for this assignment. Her whole goal is to keep both of you happy and to keep me informed. You will share her. Do not have sex with any other person, as we do not need any mishaps. Elwin, Tiffany will be traveling with you as your personal secretary. Tiffany is to pleasure you and your cousin. Do not disappoint me.

"Elwin, you can tell the truth that you graduated from Peking University with honors. You were allowed to attend because you had the grades to do so and your father was high Chinese. You will be replacing Chew-Lee as president of SUN-TECH, headquartered in Austin, Texas. Chew-Lee has moved out of the company mansion and into a penthouse in Dallas. You will only call him when you truly need help. Once you are settled in, you will contact Mr. White, Dean of Dallas High School, and make arrangements for Peter to enroll there and finish his senior year.

"Peter, you will behave yourself. Do not volunteer for anything. If a girl asks you out, which I'm sure they will, tell her you work part-time and on weekends and are too busy. If that fails, remember, no intercourse.

"Elwin, you and Tiffany will leave this Friday. Once you are settled, you can call and we will make arrangements for your cousin to come. Now, let's meet Tiffany."

Their father clapped his hands, and Tiffany came in.

The boys were in awe. Neither had ever seen a woman so beautiful.

After introductions, their father said, "Tiffany will stay with Peter for the next two days. Elwin, do not look sad. She will be with you much longer. Now you both can leave, while Tiffany and I discuss other things."

ONE MONTH LATER

It was the last week of August, and Elwin and Peter were sitting in the SUN-TECH Mansion's library. Elwin explained to Peter that tomorrow he would be taking an entrance exam to enter Dallas High School as a senior.

"It is imperative that you get in."

THE FOLLOWING DAY

The company chauffeur, Wilson, drove Peter to the high school.

As Peter got out, Wilson said, "I'll be waiting for you outside."

Peter started walking towards the main entrance where an older gentleman stood holding the door open.

"Welcome," he said, shaking Peter's hand. "I'm Mr. White."

Walking towards a room, Mr. White said to Peter, "You will be taking tests on various subjects today. These tests will determine if you should be in your senior year."

Once in the room, Mr. White introduced Peter to Mrs. Louis, explaining that she would oversee his testing and grade them when he finishes. Mr. White explained that each test covers one subject—Math, English, Science, and Spanish—and each usually takes around an hour to complete. "When you've finished, you may leave. You will be notified of the results tomorrow, and if all goes well, you will start school in September." Mr. White left the room with a smile, saying, "I hope to see you in September."

Mrs. Louis smiled and handed him the tests, telling him to bring each test up to her desk when he completed them and she'd give him another one.

Peter finished all four tests in three hours, and Mrs. Louis was surprised to find that he'd scored perfectly on all four tests even after finishing so quickly.

As Peter was walking out, Mrs. Louis said, "See you in September!"

As Peter got into the car, Wilson said, "Now for your driving permit. Everything is set."

After arriving at the DMV, Peter took the written test, and after receiving his passing score, he was informed that his road test would be at 3 that afternoon.

Peter told Wilson what the lady said as he got back in the car.

Wilson said, "Great! We can have lunch, and then you can take the road test."

After lunch, they went to the location where the tests were being given and got in line with the other cars to wait their term.

One of the instructors saw their car and came over to introduce himself. He stated that he would be giving the test as he got in the car. After putting their seat belts on, the instructor told Peter what to do, and they were off.

After finishing the test, Peter parked the car.

As the instructor got out, he turned to Peter and said, "You passed! Here is your temporary license."

As Wilson walked towards Peter, he passed the instructor and held out his hand to thank him.

While driving back, Wilson said, "Now you'll be able to drive to school rather than take the school bus."

He just said, "But I have no car. And I don't think Elwin will let me take his Bentley."

They both laughed.

Wilson said, "You never know."

As they pulled up in front of the mansion, they noticed Elwin standing next to a 1970 Chevelle SS convertible in the driveway.

When they approached, Elwin said, "Congratulations Peter! Here is your own fully restored 1970 Chevelle SS convertible. I hope you like it."

Peter replied, "I sure do! Thank you very much!"

Elwin replied, "It's my pleasure. Dad and Mom said drive safe, be careful, and always stop at stop signs."

Everyone smiled as they walked into the mansion.

SCHOOL

September came fast and before Peter knew it, he was sitting in his first class, waiting for the instructor to come in. He was surprised when he saw Mrs. Louis sit down in the front of the class.

She greeted the class, and after a few minutes students started drifting in.

While waiting, Peter reviewed his schedule. *Not bad*, he said to himself.

Math, 8 - 8:45

English, 9 - 9:45

Chemistry, 10 - 10:45

Spanish, 11 - 11:45

Lunch, 12 - 12:45

Earth Science, 1 - 1:45

Social Studies, 2 - 2:45

Gym, 3 - 3:45

The 8 o'clock school bell rang, bringing him back to reality. Mrs. Louis told the what she expected and what she would not tolerate.

Before he knew it, it was lunch time. Peter headed towards the cafeteria, and found to his pleasant surprise that lunch was free. After getting two slices of pizza, an apple, and a bottle of water, he looked for a table, noticing an empty one far in the corner.

Once he was seated, Peter started eating his lunch. When he'd finished, he started to review his subjects until he heard a female voice say, "Is it okay if we sit here?"

Peter looked up and saw two young female students and one male student. He replied, "Sure—this is not my table."

The girl who'd spoken to him introduced herself and her friends. "My name is Alicia Diego. My girlfriend is Alex Patel, and this is Manuel Garcia."

Peter replied, "My name is Peter Walker."

After finishing lunch, they were conversing about local things in the school when they all heard a loud voice say, "Where are my three little amigos?"

Looking up, they saw an entourage of five students walking towards them. The leader stood the same size as Peter. Next to the leader were two males, a little shorter in height, and three females.

Ignoring Peter, the leader said to Alicia, "I see you found pretty boy."

Peter stood up and said, "I have a name. It's Peter Walker. Who are you?"

The tall male replied with a smile, "I'm called Briggs. My friends Bert and Kevin and I oversee the school, making sure everything is running smoothly. I called you pretty boy because every girl in this school thinks you are the most handsome guy they've ever seen. Look around. Every girl is looking at you, and unfortunately not looking at me."

Briggs turned towards Alicia, saying, "Hope you and I can get together." Then he walked away with his entourage.

Peter sat down and said, "What was that all about?"

Manual said, "Briggs has had a crush on Alicia since we were in grade school. Alicia tries to stay away from him, but he torments her any chance he can. I tried once to stop him, but he broke my nose. Since then, we try to stay away from him."

Peter said, "Well, if there is anything I can do, just let me know."

The bell rang, and everybody said so long, leaving for their next class.

Before he knew it, he was standing in his last class of the day: gym.

Peter asked the instructor if he could try out for the swim team, but he was told that it was too late in the year. Instead, he could be an alternate. Peter agreed, and the rest of the gym time was just walking around the track.

The bell rang, ending Peter's first day of school.

At dinner, Peter told Elwin and Tiffany about the incident at lunch. Elwin informed Peter that Alicia is the granddaughter of Senator Diego.

Elwin explained that he works with the senator very closely, bringing in immigrants. "Senator Diego feels that the more Mexicans that come across the border makes Texas a more Mexican State. Thus, Texas is predominantly Mexican. He is unaware that for all the Mexicans that come in, we bring our Chinese citizens in as well. Make sure you take care of his granddaughter," he said before adding, "without getting yourself in trouble."

The following day at lunch, Peter waited at the same table for his new friends to join him, but they never showed.

Briggs came in and sat down in front of Peter, asking where his three amigos were.

Peter replied he did not know.

Briggs stared at him and said, "I hope you are not lying."

Peter replied, "I don't lie, and if I am, you know where to find me."

Briggs just smiled and left with his friends.

Peter sat there wondering himself where his new friends were.

As the months flew by, Peter never saw his new friends at lunch or even in school.

Before he knew it, it was November. He would be turning 18 on the 16th, and his cousin Elwin would be 22 on the 17th. Tiffany would not tell them her birthday or her age, so they said they would celebrate her birthday on the 18th with no questions asked about her age.

SWIM MEET

It was December, and Dallas High School had made it to the state swim finals. Peter sat on the bench with the rest of the team as the alternate.

Peter was wondering if he would ever get to swim, when he heard the coach yell, "Walker! Alan slipped and hurt his hand. You're taking his place. Now let's see if Mr. White was correct about how good you are."

Peter suddenly realized why the coach disliked him. Mr. White forced him to put him on the team.

It was a tough tournament, but Dallas was now tied for the championship finals. Peter proved himself more than once during the tournament. But in order for his school to win the championship, he would have to get first in the two-hundred-yard free style.

Peter stood at the edge of the pool, looking at the water and waiting patiently. He could hear the girls in the background screaming that they wanted to marry him or take him home. Then he heard the whistle.

As soon as he entered the pool, he started swimming like his life depended on it. He blanked out the noise and concentrated on his strokes.

Before he knew it, the whistle was blowing. He looked up and everybody was jumping up and down, screaming, "We won! We won!"

Peter jumped out of the pool, and everybody ran to him saying, "You did it! We won the state championship!"

The team was put in front of the podium with the trophy.

As pictures were being taken, Peter said, "Please wait a minute." He ran to the locker room and reemerged with Alan. Peter said, "Now you can take pictures—the whole team is here."

Everyone yelled and cheered until they thought they thought the roof would fall in.

When Peter entered the mansion later that night, everyone was waiting in the hall, and they all hollered, "Congratulations!"

Peter stood stunned for a few seconds.

Elwin stepped forward and said, "We heard on the daily news that the school had won the state championship and you were the lead swimmer. Congratulations! I told Mr. White you should be put on swimming team. Glad he took my advice."

Fen, the cook, said, "Come, I made you dinner."

The maids, Qiao and Qing, said, "After dinner, we will make you a hot bath."

As everyone walked away, Tiffany smiled and whispered in Peter's ear, "And I will give you dessert."

For Peter it was a great day.

GRADUATION PICTURE

The months flew by and before he knew it, it was the middle of May. The tests were done, and pictures for the yearbook were being taken.

Peter sat waiting to be called for his picture to be taken, thinking about the three young students he'd had lunch with on his first day. When his name was called, Peter sat in the chair and the photographer told him which way to pose.

A very pretty young woman walked in and asked the photographer, "May I have a moment to speak to Peter?"

He replied, "Sure. I need a smoke break anyway."

As she walked over to Peter, she said, "Remember me?"

Peter replied, "Not really, but I do think we've met somewhere."

Smiling, she replied, "We did one time at lunch. My name is Alex Patel. I felt that we owed you an explanation for why we never came back. We knew that Briggs would never leave us alone, but we also knew you would protect us from him and his gang. So we went to Mr. White and asked if we could have our lunch in an empty classroom, come in early and leave early, making it hard for Briggs to harass us. Of course Mr. White agreed." She said, "I thought you would like to know." Then she turned and started walking to the door.

Peter said, "Thank you. Are you going to the prom?"

She turned and said, "No," then shut the door.

Peter sat there thinking about what had just happened when the photographer said, "Ready?"

After the pictures were taken, the sales pitch came. Peter took the best package, paid in advance, and then left for his next class. On his way, he met Briggs in the hall, who asked, "Any chance you've seen my amigos?"

Peter replied, "Nope," and kept walking.

PROM DAY

———————

The Saturday of the prom, Elwin, Tiffany, and Peter sat having breakfast, when Elwin asked, "Peter, how come you're not going to the prom?"

Peter replied, "I told everyone I had a girlfriend, but she could not make it. I remembered what father said, and I'd rather not take any unnecessary chances to anger our father."

After finishing breakfast, Elwin said, "Tiffany and I are going over to Senator Diego's house to discuss some issues. We will be there for a while, so enjoy yourself."

Elwin and the senator were having a discussion when the senator's wife came into the room upset. She said that their granddaughter's date for the prom had cancelled and now she was upstairs crying because she did not want to go to the prom alone.

After thinking a moment, Elwin said, "I might be able to help. My cousin Peter is in the same graduating class as your granddaughter, and he wasn't going to the prom. Let me call him. I'm sure he will take her."

The senator replied, "I would be extremely grateful."

Elwin replied, "It is my honor." He turned to Tiffany and said, "Go up and talk to her. Tell her not to worry." Elwin then called Peter.

Peter was sitting by the pool and thinking about what else he had to do to complete his entrance into the Texas National Guard when his phone rang. Noticing it was Elwin, Peter answered, saying, "Everything okay?"

Elwin replied, "Yes. There's no time to explain, but you're going to the prom. Go into my closet and find my white dinner jacket. I believe your partner is wearing pink, so grab a pink shirt. You'll have to use your own black pants, but grab a nice set of cufflinks. The bowtie is a clip-on. Wilson is on his way to pick you up. He will be with you for the rest of the night. See you soon." Then he hung up.

Tiffany knocked on the senator's granddaughter's bedroom door and introduced herself as a friend of her grandparents. She then informed the senator's granddaughter that a date was coming over to take her to the prom.

The granddaughter replied, "Really? Who?"

Tiffany replied, "A young man named Walker."

The senator's granddaughter said, "Is he graduating this year too?"

Tiffany replied, "Yes."

The granddaughter jumped up and said, "I don't believe it! I'm going to the prom with the most handsome boy in our school! Hurry, I need to get my makeup and hair fixed before he gets here!"

While Tiffany was fixing the granddaughter's hair, she asked, "Did you mean what you said before?"

The granddaughter said, "Oh yes. Every girl in our school has a crush on him! I believe that some of the teachers do too!"

Tiffany started to feel a little jealous. She said to herself, *I must not have these feelings.*

PROM NIGHT

———————

While riding in the car, Peter asked, "Why did your date not show up?"

Alicia replied, "Briggs threatened Manuel that he would beat him up if he brought me."

Alicia and Peter entered the ballroom.

The music stopped playing and their names were announced, then the band started playing again. Alicia saw her table and they walked over to it. After introductions, Peter said, "I'll get us something to drink. Does anyone want one?"

They all replied, "No, thank you."

Peter came back with a drink for Alicia, then said, "Care to dance?"

They danced the night away before realizing it was 10 o'clock. The dance was going to end at 11.

As she sat down, Alicia said, "Peter would you please get me a soda?"

When Peter came back with the drinks, he saw Alicia with Briggs.

Alicia's friend at the table said, "When you left, he came over and pulled her out of the chair and said, 'Let's dance.'"

Peter put the drinks down and started walking toward Alicia. As he got close to them, Alicia pulled away from Briggs and slapped him in the face. Briggs raised his hand in anger.

Peter said, "Don't," in a voice that was so cold Briggs stopped in mid-air. Peter said to Alicia, "Go back to the table." He looked Briggs in the eyes, and smiling, he said, "Do you want to try to hit me?"

Briggs said, "Not now, pretty boy," and walked back to his group.

Peter sat next to Alicia, telling everyone that everything is okay.

Alicia said, "He called me a Mexican slut and said he would be doing me a favor if he had sex with me."

Peter said, "In time he will regret what he said. For now, go the ladies' room and freshen up, then meet me in front of the stage. I have a surprise for you."

Peter walked up to the band leader and said, "If I may, I would like to sing my girlfriend a song." He handed him $500.

The band leader said, "Sure! What song do you want to sing?"

Peter said, "'Sounds Like Something I'd Do.' May I use a guitar?"

The band leader said, "Sure. Let us know when you're ready."

Peter stood in front of the mic and spoke.

"Hi, my name is Peter Walker, and I would like to play a song as a graduation gift for my girlfriend, Alicia. I would also like to congratulate Briggs for coming out of the closet. I'm not sure, but for the past year, Briggs has been calling me 'pretty boy,' and I always see him and his two male friends, Burt and Kevin, together. Let's give them a hand either way!"

Everyone started laughing, and clapping.

Briggs and his friends got up and left.

Peter said, "Thank you," then he started singing.

The whole room went quiet.

When he finished, the entire crowd cheered and applauded.

Peter said, "Thank you," then he turned to the band and thanked them. The crowd wanted more, but Pete said, "I would like to have time with my girlfriend."

Again the crowd clapped.

When Peter got close to Alicia, she ran up to him and kissed him, saying, "Thank you! That was the best graduation gift anyone could have ever given me."

The band leader announced that this would be the last dance. "So let's get everyone up and dancing!"

As Alicia and Peter were leaving the prom, Peter asked Alicia, "Where to next?"

Alicia replied, "To Kelly's Dance Hall!"

Peter could not believe the size of the dance hall. The room had tables with benches along the wall. At one end was the stage, on the other end was the food stand, and the center was a dance floor that could hold at least 200 people.

As Peter was taking in the view, Alicia tugged his arm and started leading him to a table where her friends were. After the introductions, the girls said, "We will be right back."

About twenty minutes later, the girls came out of the restroom in dungaree shorts, high blouses, and cowboy boots.

Alicia walked up to Peter, saying, "Surprise! We all have lockers since we come here often."

They both started laughing. Peter smiled and said, "I must say, the outfits are very easy on the eyes."

At 3 am, the band leader said, "This is the last dance."

Peter looked at Alicia and said, "I can truly say we danced the night away!"

They laughed as they walked back to the table.

Alicia said, "I will right back. I have to change."

About forty-five minutes later, they stood in the front of the senator's house. Peter said, "I hope you had a good time."

Alicia looked up at him and said, "This is was best night of my life, and probably always will be." She reached up and kissed him, then walked inside, saying, "See you at graduation!"

Later on, Peter fell into his bed and immediately fell asleep.

He woke up to a knock on the door and someone saying, "Dinner is ready!"

Peter jumped up looked at his watch, saying to himself, "Wow, it's 5 o'clock. I slept the whole day away." He took a shower then went down to have dinner with Tiffany and Elwin.

While eating, Elwin and Tiffany asked Peter questions about the evening. Peter told them about the evening and the bit of trouble with Briggs.

Elwin said, "I don't see a problem yet, but if the senator finds out, Briggs, Sr. may have trouble with the big trucking company he owns."

Peter said, "Well, let's hope he doesn't find out." Peter then said, "Excuse me while I go up and pass out again on this full stomach."

RECRUITING STATION

It was early Monday morning and Peter had just finished up with the recruiter before heading towards the department store when he came face to face with Briggs and his group.

Briggs said to Burt and Kevin, "Grab him!"

But before they could grab him, Peter broke their noses. He turned to Briggs and said, "I'm waiting."

Briggs turned and started to walk away, but he saw his father looking over at him from across the street. He turned quickly back around and charged.

When he was close enough, Peter hit Briggs square in the nose, breaking it, while saying, "This is for Manuel!" Then Peter hit him in the jaw, breaking the bone, and said, "This is for insulting Alicia!" Peter stood over the three of them and said, "Want to try again? Get up."

No one moved.

Peter stepped over them and got into his car, heading to the department store.

It was late in the afternoon when Elwin called Peter. "We have a guest who would like to speak to you. We are in the library."

Peter walked into the library and saw the man that was watching his fight with Briggs from across the street.

Elwin said, "This is Mr. Briggs, Sr. He would like to ask you a few questions."

Mr. Briggs looked at Peter and said, "Why?"

Peter then informed him of his son's behavior to the girls and boys in school. He explained that when his son tried to beat him up earlier, Peter decided to let them have a taste of their own medicine.

Mr. Briggs stood up, thanked everyone, and left.

Elwin said, "What was that all about?"

Peter replied, "Nothing. I'm going to the pool and then bed. See you tomorrow."

Elwin replied, "Okay."

GRADUATION DAY

It was a beautiful day for graduation. After everyone received their diplomas, they threw their hats up into the air.

The senator asked Elwin and Tiffany to come to his house for Alicia's party.

They said, "Sure!" Laughing, they said, "Should we bring Peter too?"

Laughing, the senator said, "Sure! See you at 3."

Later, Elwin pulled up to the front of the senator's house and noticed three valets parking cars. He turned to Tiffany and said, "Can't wait to see the college graduation party!"

Peter was talking to Alicia and Manuel when Alex came in, looking beautiful. Alex came right over to them and kissed everyone.

Peter said, "I have to leave now. I'm leaving early tomorrow for the Army."

The girls started crying,

Peter said, "Don't cry! I'll be back."

As Peter wiped her tears away, Alicia said, "Would you please sing one song? Alex doesn't believe you can sing, and I told the band leader."

Laughing, Peter said, "Okay, but then I have to go."

Peter stood in front of the mic and said, "Everyone having a good time?"

The crowd yelled, "Yes!"

"Great! I'm going to sing a song that all of us have done at one time." He started singing 'Sounds Like Something I'd Do.'

Elwin looked at Tiffany. They both said at the same time, "He sings?"

When Peter finished, the crowd clapped and started cheering, "We want another song!"

Peter said, "Okay, but this will be the last song!" He then started singing 'Your Man.'

The crowd went crazy. When he finished, the crowd cheered for about five minutes. Peter thanked the band and everyone, then said, "Bless you all! May you all a have a good life!"

Peter walked to the front door, waved, then left.

When Peter came down the steps the following morning, Elwin and Tiffany were waiting for him.

Elwin said, "You know, Father is going to be very angry. Why are you doing this?"

Peter replied, "If I'm going to enter politics, this will be in my favor."

Elwin replied, "Please don't do this."

Peter said, "It's too late. I have a cab waiting for me. I will call the first chance I get." Peter hugged them both then left.

BOOT CAMP

It was his first day as a recruit in Fort Benning, Georgia, and the drill sergeant was yelling cadence as they marched. The men joined in with the singing, and that night, Peter fell asleep singing 'Jody' in his mind.

The ten weeks went by fast. Before he knew it, he was graduating as the top soldier of his class.

The commander requested Peter join him in his office. Once in his office, the commander said, "You asked to join the Rangers. While it is highly unusual for a reservist, you surpassed all the requirements. You have a choice. Tomorrow they're starting the session here. Do you want it?"

Without hesitation, Peter said, "Yes."

The commander told Peter what to expect.

The course was sixty-one days long and was given in three phases:

1. Benning phase

2. Mountain phase

3. Swamp phase

"Should you fail in any of these phases, you must wait a year before trying again. Should you pass, you must drill in Fort Benning for your reserve."

Peter said, "Thank you."

After leaving the commander's office, Peter called Elwin and give him an update.

Elwin replied that his parents were worried for his safety.

Peter thanked him, but said, "I have to go."

Training seven days a week, eighteen hours a day, the sixty-one days went by fast.

After graduating, Peter was ordered to the commander's office where he stood at attention, saying, "Reporting, as ordered, sir."

The commander replied, "At ease. Peter, you have been excellent soldier. You are one of six reservists that completed the ranger course. As you know this a pilot program for Reserves. I'm offering you a chance to go to OCS. It is a twelve-week course. We could use leaders like you. It is your decision. Your training would be here at Fort Benning. The course starts tomorrow. What is your answer?"

Peter replied, "Thank you for this opportunity, sir. Where do I report?"

After leaving the commander's office, Peter called Elwin and told him of his decision.

Elwin said that Peter was very foolish and should be careful

Peter assured Elwin that he was doing what was best. "Give my love to Tiffany." Before Elwin could say anything, Peter hung up.

As Peter shook the commander's hand while accepting his lieutenant bars, Peter thought about how fast time flew by. Maybe it was because they gave him no time for his mind to wander or be idle.

Peter stopped by to see Alicia but was told that she was out with Alex, so he headed home. When he opened the front door, everyone was waiting for him. They had a big sign that said: Welcome Home! Tiffany, Penny, and the maids ran to him, grabbing and hugging him. When they were done crying and hugging him, Elwin stepped forward shook his hand, saying, "Welcome home." Then he hugged him.

After having a delicious meal made especially for him, Peter said, "Elwin, before I go up and change, may we talk privately in the library?"

Peter explained to Elwin that his main reason for joining the Army was to see how their special forces compared to theirs. Peter found them to be excellent. "Equal to the People's Liberation Army. The Americans' main power is their camaraderie." He also stated, "When the time comes to run for politics, being an Army veteran will be a plus."

He then got up. "I truly missed you cousin, but not as much as I missed Tiffany."

When Peter entered his bedroom, Tiffany was waiting with a smile. She said, "Miss me?"

While lying in bed, Tiffany said to Peter, we knew you played the guitar, but we didn't know you could sing!"

Peter replied, "I wasn't sure either but that night at the prom, I had to do something to get Alicia's mind off what Briggs had said to her or she would have told her grandfather, and that might cause a bigger problem. I figured, what the heck, this is where I can find out if I can sing or not."

After taking a shower together, while drying each other off, Tiffany said, "I hope you remember, today is New Year's Eve. We will be attending the senator's party. Are you coming?"

Peter replied, "I think not. I'm sure Alicia is mad at me for not writing or calling. I think I'll just hang here and swim in the pool."

While leaving the room, Tiffany said, "Okay. We will be leaving early, but your cousin hopes to see you there."

NEW YEAR'S EVE

The house was quiet. Peter guessed all the staff was off. As he dove into the pool, he heard his name being called. Looking up, he saw Alicia and Alex. He started swimming towards the steps. When he got out and started drying off, he started saying to Alicia, "I know I was wrong. Sorry—"

But Alicia did not want to hear that. She walked up to him and starting yelling, "You has some nerve not calling me!"

Before Peter could apologize, Alicia said, "It doesn't matter now. Manual and I made up. If you come to the party, find yourself another girlfriend." Then she turned and started walking out.

Alex said, "I will pick you up at 8," then turned and ran to catch up to Alicia.

Peter stood there wondering what had just happened.

As he got into the car at 8 o'clock, he said, "Wow, what a beautiful Bentley!"

Alex replied, "Well, I knew you weren't going to fit in the 'vette."

As they were driving, Peter noticed that they had passed the senator's house. He turned and said, "Where are we going?"

Smiling, Alex replied, "My house. I want you to meet my family."

As they approached the house, Peter said, "Alex, is there something I should know?"

Alex replied, "No, why?"

Peter said, "Because your house is twice the size of mine and the senator's put together."

As the valets opened the doors, Alex said, "It is just a house. My family is Chinese and Spanish. We manufacture all types of Chinese and Mexican food. Is that a problem?"

Peter replied, "No, but you don't look Chinese."

Smiling, Alex said, "Thank you. You should be honored that you are the first non-Hispanic or Chinese I brought home. If we marry out of our blood line, we will be disowned. You are the first man I met that I may be willing to do so."

Peter said, "What?"

At that moment, they reached the front of the house. There were guards with clipboards checking names. Alex walked right in and got lost in the crowd.

The guard stopped Peter and said, "Name please."

Peter replied, "Peter Walker."

The guard said, "Sorry, sir, your name is not on the list."

Peter said, "Okay. When Miss Patel comes out, please tell her that I'm at the closest bar," then turned and walked away.

As he walked into the bar, he noticed that it was not that crowded. Walking up to the bar, he said, "Is the kitchen still open?"

The barmaid replied, "For you, handsome, everything is open."

Peter said, "Great—may I have the biggest steak you have—medium well—and potatoes."

The barmaid replied, "We have a 72 ounce. If you finish it, no charge. If you don't, $100. Just to let you know, 150 people have failed."

Peter said, "Bring it out."

Everyone hearing it said, "We have to see this."

Peter had just finished and everyone was cheering when the front door of the bar opened and Alex walked in.

A male voice said, "Wow! Where'd this beautiful queen come from?"

As she walked over to Peter, Alex said, "Quiet, or I'll have your head taken off."

Everybody was watching Alex as she moved through the crowd. She stood in front of Peter and said, "Why did you leave?"

Peter replied, "Didn't have an invitation, and he wouldn't let me in."

"But you were with me."

Peter replied, "You didn't act like it."

The girls said to Alex, "Who are you?"

Alex replied, "I'm his wife."

The girls said, "Oh, he didn't say he was married."

Peter replied, "I just found out myself."

Alex said to Peter, "Please come back home with me. My family is waiting to meet you."

Peter sat there for a few moments, then said, "Sorry ladies. My wife has spoken." He then took out $400 and put it on the bar, saying, "Drinks on me—Happy New Year."

Alex walked around with Peter, introducing him to her family. It was almost midnight when Alex said, "Let's dance!"

They were dancing when the countdown started. Then at midnight, everyone yelled, "Happy New Year!" and Peter gently took Alex by her waist, picked her up, and kissed her.

Alex felt like the world had stopped. The kiss lasted longer than either of them expected, when Peter gently put her down, she looked up and said, "What are you looking for?"

Peter replied, "A woman to love that is loyal and a virgin."

Alex said, "Why must she be a virgin?"

Peter replied, "I could never look at her, knowing that another man had made love to her. I could even meet him some day, and he might say, 'I made love to your wife.'"

Alex said, "Doesn't it matter that she loves you and no one else?"

Peter replied, "No," then walked away.

Alex said, "Where are you going?"

Peter said, "Home. I have a lot to do."

Alex said, "Then let me take you home."

When they got to Peter's house, he got out of the car and reached into his pocket, taking out three small, wrapped boxes. "For the three amigos. Merry Christmas."

Alex held them in her hand and said, "May I open mine?"

Peter replied, "Sure."

Alex opened her present and saw a bracelet. On the bracelet, it said, *To my three amigos*. She turned it over and it read, *Love, Gringo*.

Alex's eyes began to moisten. She got out of the car, ran up to him, and hugged him. "Peter, please don't push me away."

Peter looked down and said, "Alex, you are a very beautiful woman. A man could fall in love with you very easily. But I cannot be that man now."

Alex got into the car crying and left.

Elwin and Peter sat talking about where his future was going.

Elwin, with sadness in his voice, said, "The more powerful I get, the further you must be from me."

Peter replied, "I will miss you cousin, but it is for our people."

Elwin said, "You will still see Tiffany once a month, and we can still meet occasionally, but we have to be subtle about it. I know that Alex Patel is romantically interested in you, but please remember that her father plays an important role when the time comes. Please don't push her too far away."

Peter replied, "I understand, cousin. I'll be going to Texas Law School in Austin. This will make it easier for me to get to my drills in El Paso. My research found a log cabin with a pond and barn nearby. It sits on 20 acres of land that I will be able to rent for four years from an elderly lady name Wheatly.

"Mrs. Wheatly said that the cabin was once used as bed and breakfast, but it was getting to be too much for her. I told her that I would fix anything that breaks. I'm paying her a fair rent. It is a little out of the way from school, but that is the way I like it."

Elwin said, "Sounds great. It's my understanding that Alex wants to be an architect and interior designer and will be going to a school in Houston. Alicia and Manuel will be going to the University of Texas at Dallas for business."

Peter replied, "That is great—they won't be too close to me but close enough to meet if they wish. School doesn't start til January 21, so that'll give me time to fix up the log cabin the way I like. It's in excellent shape—just needs a little tender care, as they say.

"I hope you don't mind, but I asked Wilson to take care of my car. I bought a used Jeep—the road to the cabin is gravel."

He then hugged Tiffany and Elwin. Tears were beginning to form in everyone's eyes as Peter said, "Well, this it. Time to leave the nest. I will text you my address. I drill every fourth weekend."

LOG CABIN

Peter opened the front door of the cabin and found it to his liking. It was rustic and cozy. Before leaving home, Peter had had the electric turned on in his name. The oil tanks were full, and Mrs. Wheatly gave him the names of the oil company and gardener, plus all the companies she used to maintain the area.

The cabin had two bedrooms, a den, a great room with a fireplace, a gallery kitchen, a bathroom in each bedroom, a half bathroom in the hall, a deck in the rear that overlooked the lake, and a porch in the front of the house. He made the den his training room where he could lift weights and practice his karate.

COLLEGE

Peter was a little nervous about what to expect the first day of college, but once things got going, he fell into a routine.

The first thing was orientation. They told him all about campus events and activities, such as intramural sports. The orientation leader also talked about how to use the cafeteria's meal plan. "In addition, you might also want to take advantage of some of the other programs available on your campus. This is a great way to meet new people!"

After orientation, he went to registration. With his schedule, Peter would be able to get 18 credits per semester, allowing him to get a juris degree in three years. Once he passed the bar exam, he could practice law in Texas.

Each month, he would drill on the fourth weekend, see Tiffany on the third weekend, meet up with the three amigos on the second weekend every other month, and train or study on free weekends. Time was like a blur. Everything was going fast.

Peter found a new friend while drilling. The Army was retiring a canine named King. He was very big, and nobody was really interested in taking him. Peter took him, saying to himself, *It does get lonely every once in a while up in the cabin without Tiffany, and King will make great company,* which turned out to be true.

By the end of Peter's third year, he had completed all of the requirements to take the bar exam.

To celebrate, he met his friends at everyone's favorite café. As he approached the table and sat down, he only saw Alicia and Manue. As he sat, Peter said, "I guess Alex couldn't make it. Is she doing a fashion show?"

Alicia replied, "Alex said not to say anything because you've been so busy, but she was attacked about two months ago. She thinks it was Briggs. He cut her face pretty badly. All she does sit in her room; she refuses to come out."

Peter said, "What did they do to Briggs?"

Alicia said, "Nothing—he had a rock-solid alibi."

Peter got up from the table, saying, "I'm going to see her."

Alicia said, "She refuses to see anybody, Peter."

Peter replied, "She'll see me whether she likes it or not."

Peter rang Mr. Patel's doorbell, and the maid came to the door. "Can I help you?"

Peter replied, "I want to speak to Alex."

The maid said, "She has refused to come out or let anyone in her room."

Peter barged past the maid, saying, "Well, she's going to see me." He ran up the steps three at a time, and when he got to Alex's room, he knocked on the door and said, "Alex, can I please come in?"

In a crying voice, she said, "No—I don't want you to see me this way."

Peter said, "Tough. I'm coming in."

He kicked the door in, and Alex quickly covered her face. She said, "You have no right to come in here."

Peter said, "I have every right. You love me, and I love you. It's just not the right time to get married."

Alex said, "You love me? But you said you would only marry a virgin."

Peter looked at her and asked, "Are you?"

Alex said, "Yes, but love should be the only reason to marry someone."

Peter replied, "Well, now we have both. Let me see your face."

Alex slowly removed the sheet.

Peter said, "Well, it did scar your beauty, but I'm sure plastic surgery will repair that. Did he cut you anyplace else?"

Alex held up her arm and showed him a long scar.

Peter said, "Plastic surgery can fix that too. So why are you hiding?"

Alex replied, "I don't want anyone to see me like this. Besides, Briggs may attack me again."

Peter said, "Pack your things. You're coming with me. I'll take care of Briggs."

Alex started packing while crying. "Please don't do anything foolish!"

Peter said, "Don't worry, I won't. Are you ready?"

Alex said, "Yes, but where are we going?"

Peter replied, "Where you can relax, have no reporters sneaking around and feel safe. When you feel ready, we'll go get the best that we can find."

On the way to the cabin, Peter stopped at a 7-11 and bought a couple burner phones. He gave one to Alex and said, "Just put your parents' number and Alicia's number in, then give me your phone."

Peter took her phone, broke it in half, and threw it in the garbage.

On the way to the cabin, Peter asked Alex, "Why did Briggs attack you?"

Alex replied, "Because he thinks I told Alicia to stay away from him, which I did."

It was late afternoon when they arrived at the cabin. Before going in, Peter said to Alex, "I hope you aren't afraid of dogs, because I have one."

Laughing, Alex said, "I love dogs."

Peter opened the door to find King sitting and wagging his tail.

Alex saw him and ran right over. She started hugging him and kissing him, saying, "He is very big and handsome like you."

Peter stood there saying to himself, *Does King know she is hurt, and that's why he's letting her hug him?* Aloud, Peter said, "Alex, let me show you to your bedroom. You can lie down and rest while I make us something to eat."

Alex said, "You cook? Wow, you never cease to amaze me."

Peter just smiled, and turning to King, said, "Protect Alex."

King barked once.

Peter turned to Alex and explained, "One bark means yes, two barks means no. Please rest. I'll come get you when dinner is ready."

Peter stepped out on the porch where he called Wilson. "Would you please find out where Briggs hangs out? Don't tell anyone I asked."

Wilson replied, "I shouldn't, but that guy needs a good beating and I know you're going to give it to him. Okay. I'll find out."

Peter said, "Great," then hung up.

The week went by fast. Alex was healing quickly and getting her strength back. She'd never been so happy.

At dinner, she said, "Peter, can we stay here forever?"

Peter smiled and said, "Someday, maybe."

Just then, Peter's burner phone buzzed. He picked it up and saw a text from Wilson.

Alex said, "Who is it?"

Peter replied, "Just spam."

While they were eating on Saturday evening, Peter put sleeping power in Alex's drink. By six o'clock, Alex yawned and said, "Peter, please excuse me. I must go to bed; I feel very tired."

Peter said, "No problem. Here, let me help you."

Once in bed, Peter kissed her goodnight.

Sometime later, Peter sat patiently waiting in a dark parking lot, dressed in all black to blend in with the darkness.

Around 2 AM, Briggs came out of the bar with a girl. As they walked to their car, Briggs kept kissing and trying to feel her breasts. The woman got into the car, saying, "Now I have to fix my makeup!"

Laughing, Briggs started to open his car door when he felt a hand on his shoulder. He turned to see who it was, and that was the last thing he remembered. Peter hit him in the nose, breaking it. He hit Briggs' jaw, breaking it. As Briggs fell to the ground, Peter stomped on his hand, crushing every bone, then stomped down on his knee, crushing the knee cap. Finally, before walking away, Peter lifted his leg high and stomped Briggs' manhood.

As Peter walked away, he could hear the car radio blasting and the girl hollering for Briggs to hurry up.

Peter got into the car and thanked Wilson for helping. They drove for a few miles before stopping. Peter undressed, putting everything into a paper bag. Wilson then drove Peter to the front of his property. When Peter got out, he thanked Wilson again for his help, to which Wilson replied, "My pleasure. I will burn the clothes." Then he took off.

Peter, wearing only his shorts, ran to the cabin. Once inside, he took a quick shower and fell into bed, smiling.

The next morning, while having a late breakfast, Alex said, "I've never felt so tired before."

Laughing, Peter said, "It must be the country air."

Just then, there was a knock on the door.

Peter said, "I'll get it."

He opened the door.

The man standing there said, "I'm Detective Lawson. May I have a moment of your time?"

Peter said, "Sure."

Detective Lawson said, "Where were you last night?"

Peter asked, "Why?"

Detective Lawson said, "Because Mr. Briggs was attacked last night. He is in critical but stable condition, and your name was mentioned."

Peter said, "I was here all night."

Detective Lawson said, "Can you prove it?"

Peter hesitated for a moment.

Then Alex came to the door. "Yes, he can. He was home with me."

Detective Lawson said, "Who are you?"

"My name is Alex Patel."

Detective Lawson said, "Mr. Walker, do you own a pair of sneakers?"

When Peter said yes, Detective Lawson said, "May I see them?"

Peter went and got a pair of white sneakers, showing them to the detective. "Is there a problem?"

The detective said, "No. We found bloody sneaker footprints. May I come in and look around your house?"

Peter replied, "Sure," and stepped aside to let him in.

Detective Lawson said, "Is that dog safe?"

Peter replied, "Yes, he is… until I say otherwise."

After inspecting the whole house, Detective Lawson thanked them both and left.

Alex turned to Peter when they were alone and said, "Did you do that to Briggs?"

Peter replied, "Ask me no questions, and I shall tell you no lies. When are you leaving for New York to get the plastic surgery done?"

While heading to the bedroom, Alex said, "Today. A car is picking me up this afternoon. Peter, I hope you didn't hurt Briggs. You could ruin your whole life!"

Peter replied, "You *are* my life." He walked over, picked her up, and kissed her.

Alex said, "You've got to stop doing that. You make my head spin!"

They both laughed as she walked into the bedroom.

Alex came out of the bedroom with her bags packed and King next to her. "I'll be taking King with me. I'll be gone for three to four months. After the surgery, I have two photoshoots."

A car honked outside.

"I have to go. Wish me luck," she said as she and King opened the front door. "I love you… please don't do any foolish. And keep in touch."

Three weeks later, Peter passed his bar exam.

Next step, a year in the Army. He would be stationed in El Paso.

Peter called and asked Mrs. Wheatly if he could buy the cabin.

When she said yes, Peter said, "Great! I will draw up the papers before I leave."

Mrs. Wheatly said, "Okay. Make sure you put down that it's a gift."

Peter replied, "That is very generous of you—are you sure?"

"Everything anyone owns is actually rented as we cannot bring it home with us," she replied. "Someone else will eventually use it, and I would like you to be the one."

Peter replied, "I cannot thank you enough, Mrs. Wheatly." Just then there was a knock on the cabin door. "I have to go. Thank you again."

He hung up, and when he opened the door, Mr. Briggs and two very large men stood on the threshold.

Mr. Briggs asked, "Peter, these two guys are going to do to you what you did to my son."

Peter said, "First of all, Mr. Briggs, I'm not worried about those two guys because you will be the first one I kill. But before this escalates any further, you should know that the police have already questioned me and inspected every inch of my home. Besides, I have a rock-solid alibi."

With that, Peter stepped back, readying himself to strike.

Briggs stood silent for a moment, then turned and left with his men.

EL PASO ARMY BASE

"Good morning, Commander. Lieutenant Walker, reporting for duty."

Commander Cusumano replied, "Welcome! I've heard great things about you. Your squad should be here by tomorrow. It will consist of three green berets reserves. They, same as you, will drill for one year. So far, Staff Sergeant Mike Vitello is the only one here. Sergeant Charles Wolfinger and Specialist Bill Miller will arrive tomorrow. For now, familiarize yourself with the camp, and I'll see you and your team at 1300 tomorrow. Good day. Please shut the door on your way out."

At 1300 the next day, Walker and his team were sitting in the briefing room when Commander Cusumano walked in. Everybody stood at attention.

The commander said, "Sit. What I'm about to tell you is highly classified, and the only people who know is high command and us. Your mission is to enter Mexico and eliminate a group of slave traders that has been treating the migration line like a shopping mall for young women, men, and children to use as slaves. Our intelligence tells us that this group is not the cartel, but a group that feel it is easy money. Any questions?"

"Yes, sir," replied Lieutenant Walker.

"What is your question?" replied the commander.

Walker replied, "Do we know where they come from? Know their hideout? Do we know when they strike?"

The commander said, "No, that's up to you to find out. We do know that they attack the migration line long before it gets close to the United States border, but that's all we know. You leave tomorrow at 0800. Bring enough supplies for several days. We will be giving you the latest all-terrain vehicles. Come back safe."

At 0800, Walker and his team stood watching as the four ATVs were loaded onto the truck. The trucker took them to an isolated location.

After the vehicles were unloaded, Peter said, "From here on, we only speak Spanish—no rank, first names only. Any questions?"

Charles said, "What is our team's name?"

Vito said, "Let's call ourselves the Angels of Death. We are doing good, right?"

Walker said, "If we're all in agreement, so be it. Now, let's go."

MEXICO

They rode out of sight of the migration line. When they reached the end of the line, they set up battle positions and waited. The wait wasn't long before two trucks and a car were spotted.

Walker said, "Okay. I see two men on each truck bed and two in each cab. Can't see the men in the car. Remember: we need at least one alive. Miller, take out the car with the rocket. Charles, take out the first truck—do cab first, then the men on back. Mike, you take out the men in cab of second truck, and I will take care of men on the back of the truck. They're stopping. Fire now!"

Within seconds, all but one of the enemies were dead. The survivor jumped off the truck and hid behind the bed.

Peter told Miller to put a speaker on the drone then fly it 3 clicks from here to the last man standing. Once the drone was over the man, Peter said, "Put your hands up and come out. We are not going to shoot you. We want you to give a message to your boss."

The man came out with his hands up.

Peter said, "Take your phone out and call your boss."

The man did not move.

Peter shot him in the leg. "Call your boss."

The man picked up the phone and dialed. He then held the phone out as the drone dropped lower near the man.

Through the speaker on the drone, Peter spoke into the phone. "I don't care who you are. Leave our product alone. If you don't, we will kill you and family." Peter then told the man to put the phone in the basket on the drone and start walking.

When they could no longer see the man, Mike and Charles rode down and took everything out of the pockets of the dead men. They then moved the trucks and set them on fire before returning to camp.

Peter said, "We have to move camp and prepare for attack. Bill, send the information from the phones back to headquarters—they can figure out who is behind this from the info in the SIM cards. Now let's move, then dig in."

Two days passed with no sign of the enemy.

Mike said, "Maybe they aren't coming."

Peter just smiled. "They are coming."

Just then they heard a loud noise. Peter looked through his binoculus and saw three trucks with 50 calibers on the rear of them and about 50 drones heading their way.

Peter shouted, "Take cover! Each of you take a rocket and take out a truck. I will be firing at the drones. Once you take out the trucks, take cover. We're about to be in a hailstorm of bullets. Bill, tell headquarters to hurry up and take out the leader or we aren't going to make it! Charles, how many rockets do we have left?"

He replied, "One."

Peter said, "Okay. Send it into the center of the drones. I will try to shoot it. That should take a lot of them down."

Peter aimed, hitting the rocket dead-center, taking out most of the drones. But it was not enough to stop the hailstorm. Then they all heard a loud boom far off in the distance, and the drones dropped to the ground.

After a few moments, Peter said, "Anyone hit?"

Bill said, "Yes. We are all hit."

Peter replied, "Bad?"

They all answered, "No."

Peter said, "Great—let's get the hell out of here. Bill, radio ahead and let them know that we're coming. Have medical there. Now let's move out."

EL PASO CAMP

It was about midday when the team arrived in camp. Getting out of the vehicle, Vitello noticed a group of beautiful women posing for photos around various military equipment. He said to the team, "Look at the welcome back we are getting!"

The team looked, saying, "What a nice welcome back!"

Peter stood there smiling, when one of the women noticed them and started towards them with a very big dog.

Charles said, "Isn't that Alex Petal, voted the most beautiful woman in the world?"

As she got closer, Miller said, "Yes! She was on the front cover of the swimsuit mag!"

By then, Alex was standing in front of them. She put her hands on her hips, looking at Peter, and said, "Well? Are you going to kiss me or not?"

Peter bent down and gently lifted her up, kissing her. He then kissed King.

All at once, the team said, "How come she didn't ask me?"

Peter introduced his team to Alex and King, then said, "Alex, your people are calling you."

Alex replied, "Let them wait. She felt a wetness on her hand and looked to see it covered in blood. Looking up at Peter, she saw his face bleeding and fainted.

Peter caught her before she hit the ground. He carried her over to her group, gently laying her down on a cot, saying to the cameraman, "When she wakes up, please tell her that I'm okay and will see her later."

Peter walked back to where his team stood wondering about what had just happened. He said, "Okay, let's go to medical and get checked out. Then you can all go relax while I check in with the commander."

After hearing Peter's report, the commander said, "You and your team did excellent. By the way, I understand you know Alex. Would you please join us at the officer's club for dinner?"

Peter replied, "I will try, but I cannot fit into my dress uniform with this bad arm."

The commander said, "Then wear your tropical dress. I'm sure the ladies would love to see those muscles. Dinner is at 6."

Everyone enjoyed their dinner. When they had finished, someone said, "Let's go to the bar for a few drinks."

Alex said, "You will have to excuse us. My husband Peter and I have some things to discuss."

The commander's wife turned to Peter and said, "You're married?"

As Peter rose from his seat, he replied, "It's new to me every time she says it."

Once outside, Peter said to Alex, "You have to stop saying that we are married."

Alex said, "I will not. I've seen those women licking their lips for you."

Peter said, "Come with me."

Alex said, "You know, any man in the world would marry me."

Peter stopped and turned to Alex. "Then marry one of them." He turned and walked away.

Alex ran after Peter, saying, "I was only teasing."

Peter turned and said, "Do you love me?"

Alex said, "Yes—with all my heart."

Peter reached into his pocket, got down on one knee, and said, "Alex, will you marry me?"

Alex jumped up and down in excitement. "Yes!"

They kissed and hugged.

Peter said, "We'll have to wait a while to get married. By the way, I did ask your father for permission.

Alex said, "Thank you for doing that!"

Peter replied, "I'm glad you're happy. Would you like to come over to the NCO club? My team is waiting. If you have three girlfriends, invite them, and we'll celebrate."

Later on, Peter introduced Alex to his team.

Alex's girlfriends arrived a few moments after them.

"I'll pair them off," Alex whispered to Peter. "Jeanette, this Mike. Charlie, this is Connie. Bill, this is Penny."

It was a night to remember for everyone.

The next morning, everyone stood in front of Alex's bus and said their so longs.

When the bus had left, Peter said, "Okay—back to training!"

A few weeks went by, and Peter received a text from Alex telling him that the cabin was full of termites and needed to be torn down. *Can I build the replacement house?* she asked.

Peter replied: *Okay… but no big mansion.*

THE LAST MISSION

Weeks turned into months, and before the team knew it, only a week remained before they would be discharged into the reserves. Sitting in the NCO club, Peter and his team were laughing and joking about what they would do when they get out. Their first priority seemed to be to look up the ladies they'd been introduced to the night of Peter's engagement.

Suddenly, Peter's phone buzzed with a text. Peter read the message and said, "Hold on, fellas. The commander wants us in his office immediately."

MEETING

Addressing the team, Commander Cusumano said, "The Mexican president's nine-year-old daughter was taken by the El Toro cartel. They want the president to release their leader in exchange for his daughter. If not, they will kill her. Little do they know that their leader has been killed by a rival gang. We must act quickly and rescue her before they find out."

The commander pulled up a blueprint of a house, displaying it on the screen. "This is where we think they are keeping the girl. Approximately 15 to 20 men are there at all times. Any suggestions?"

Peter said, "I have an idea."

RESCUE

Dressed as a priest, Peter stood in front of the gate.

The guard approached and said, "What do you want, Padre? Why do you have a phone?"

Peter said, "I am here to make sure the president's daughter is alive and well before we release your leader. The phone is to send pictures of her to her father."

The guard pulled out his radio and called for Rafael, who Peter knew from the intel file as second in command of the cartel.

After the guard relayed the priest's story, Rafael's voice came over the radio, saying, "Search him, then let him in."

After a quick pat down, Peter was able to pass. Undetected during the search, one button on his coat concealed a hidden camera. He turned around like he wasn't sure where he was going so the team could see the guards.

One of the guards said, "I can take you to where Rafael is, Padre."

Once inside the house, they led him directly to the library, where Rafael sat at his desk.

Rafael said to the guard, "Bring the girl here." A young girl was brought into the room and placed in a chair. Rafael said, "See? She is alive."

Peter walked over to the girl and said in a whisper, "Please play along." Peter said loudly, "Look at this mark! Who did this?"

Rafael said, "Where?" He walked over to the girl, and said, "I do not see a mark."

The girl pointed to the guard and said, "He did it!"

Rafael turned and shot the guard before he could say anything.

Peter quickly turned and hit Rafael hard in the nose, pushing the bone into his brain, killing him instantly. He hit the remaining guard in the throat, killing him. He then took out the phone, called his team, and said, "Now."

Peter picked up the girl, grabbed Rafael's golden gun, and started running to the front door. There was a big bang as the armored truck crashed through the gate. It pulled up in front of the house and the doors flew open. Vitello and Miller kept the enemy at bay, as Peter hurtled toward the truck with the girl.

Peter felt a sudden pain in his shoulder, then his side and leg, but his adrenaline kept him going. He jumped into the truck, and Miller closed the door.

Wolfinger turned the truck around and peeled out. When they got safe distance from the house, Vitello spoke in his phone saying, "Send the message."

All they could see was a big cloud of fire in the distance.

Miller said, "Peter, you look pretty shot up."

Peter said, "Is the girl okay?"

The girl replied, "Yes."

Peter said, "Good," then passed out.

THREE WEEKS LATER

_____

Peter woke up, just as the nurse came in. "Welcome to the land of the living, Captain Walker."

Peter said, "How long have I been here? Where are we? And I'm a lieutenant."

The nurse replied, "Three weeks. You're at the president of Mexico's house. And you were promoted to Captain while you were in a coma. Now, I will go get the doctor and let him know that you are awake. There are a lot of people who want to see you—especially your wife. We didn't know you were married. A lot of hearts were broken when she told us."

Peter replied, "It is always a surprise to me too."

The president of Mexico came in with his daughter and thanked him. "Should you ever need anything, just ask."

Next came Commander Cusumano, who informed him that he would be retired with a medical discharge. "Higher command is looking into having a special branch formed in every reserve unit."

His team came in next. "The president of Mexico wants us to stay and form a unit like ours."

The day went by fast. Peter had just closed his eyes when Tiffany and Alex came in.

As they walked toward him, he said to himself, *How lucky can I be? I have the two most beautiful women in the world by me.*

That thought quickly changed, though, when they started talking and acting like a mother.

Two days later, Peter stood in front of his team, ready to depart. They gave him a present saying it was from all of them.

Peter opened the package. It was Rafael's gold gun with "The Angels of Death" inscribed on the handle. Peter thanked them for the present and wished them all well.

When he got in the car, Alex could not stop kissing him. They reached the airport and got out of the car.

Peter said, "Whose plane is this?"

Alex said, "My family's. Let's get home—I cannot wait to show you our new home!"

After landing and driving away in another car, they pulled up to a set of gates. The driver punched in a code, and the gates opened.

Peter said, "Gates, paved roads...what's next?"

They pulled up to 4,000 square foot house. It was a contemporary mansion with a five-car garage. King sat out front, wagging his tail. Peter got out and hugged King while saying, "Alex, this isn't my taste and you know it."

Alex said, "Please let me show you first. It has 5 bedrooms, 7 bathrooms, and a pool. We found out the lake was a natural spring, so we enlarged it to 4 acres."

As they walked through the house, Alex knew Peter was not happy. While walking, they came to two big doors. Alex opened them and said, "This is your room!"

Peter was amazed. The ceilings were a least 20 feet high and the walls were lined with books with a ladder to reach each shelf. His desk looked over the lake. Peter was speechless. He turned to Alex and kissed her with passion.

Alex said, "You've got to stop that. You know you make my legs weak."

They both laughed.

Alex said to Peter, "I hope you understand that we are young. When friends come to our home, they will see a young couples' house."

Smiling, Peter replied, "Okay, you win."

Alex said, "Let's get married here with just family and a few friends."

Peter said, "Okay, how about next week?"

Alex reached up and kissed him. "Yes. Now, I must go home and prepare."

Peter said, "Aren't you staying here?"

Alex replied, "No. You can sleep in any bedroom but ours. That bedroom is for us."

THE WEDDING

————————

The bride and groom looked like movie stars. Everyone loved the house. Alex's parents were upset that they could not throw their only daughter a bigger wedding, so they gave them the house as a wedding present.

The reception was held in the backyard under a gigantic tent.

Elwin walked over to the newly married couple and introduced his most important client. "Peter, please give her the pleasure of dancing with her as I dance with your new bride."

Peter teared up as he started dancing with his mother. "Mother, coming here was very dangerous."

His mother replied, "I wouldn't miss my son's wedding for anything. Besides, I have a message from your father. He said to never put yourself in danger again, and I agree with him."

The night went by quickly. Before anyone knew it, it was time to leave.

Later that night, Alex and Peter lay together in bed.

Peter said, "Are you nervous?"

Alex replied, "No, not really."

Peter started kissing her as he gently removed her negligee. Then he started slowly moving his hand down to her womanhood. When he felt her womanhood moisten, he whispered in her ear, "Are you ready?"

Alex nodded her head.

Peter mounted her, feeling tension. He went very slowly. After a few seconds, she grabbed his buttocks, pulling him closer, saying, "Faster."

After a few more times, they fell in each other's arms, saying, "I love you."

Over the years, they fell into a routine like all married couples. They both went to work. King always went with Alex. Peter set up a law office in Austin. After a few years, his practice grew.

One night after dinner, Alex said to Peter, "I have a surprise for you."

Peter, smiling, said, "What is it?"

Alex said, "I'm pregnant."

Peter felt like someone had punched him in his heart.

Alex said, "Why are you so sad? Don't you want a child?"

Peter said, "Yes, but I was told that I couldn't make a child."

Alex stepped back and said, "Do you think I would cheat on you?" She left the office crying.

Peter tried calling Alex, but she refused to answer.

Peter went to the doctor to see if he could explain why he couldn't have children. The doctor said, "Let's do some tests to make sure."

After a few hours the doctor came back and told Peter his sperm were healthy enough to make a lot of rabbits.

Peter went to Alex's parents' house to ask permission to speak to her. He explained to them that everything had been a misunderstanding. Her father said that she had left for a photo shoot in Italy.

Peter thanked them and left. He texted Alex, explaining that he'd had an injury when he was young and had been told he could never have children and that was why he'd been upset. *But I went to the doctor and was told I could. Please forgive me. Love, Peter.*

Two months later, Peter was in his study doing some paperwork when he heard the front door open. He got up to see who it was, and when he saw Alex, he rushed to her, saying how sorry he was.

Nine months later, Alex gave birth to twins—a boy and girl.

Peter was amazed at how beautiful the babies were and at how interracial marriage makes children even more beautiful. The boy they named Peter had jet black hair, light blue eyes, and a medium complexion. His sister, named Joanne, had blonde hair, blue eyes, and a light complexion.

6 YEARS LATER

Peter was sitting in his office when his burner phone rang. He picked it up and said, "Hello?"

The voice on the other end said, "It is time to run for congress. Senator Diego is stepping down. A team will come to your office and set up your campaign schedule. Question nothing. Do as they tell you." The caller hung up.

Doing what he was told, Peter won by a landslide and was the youngest senator in history when he took office.

Over the next six years, Peter tried to do what the people of Texas wanted. With the help of Elwin's control over the media, Peter was received well throughout the United States. A lot of people called him the next Kenny. Elwin made sure pictures of Peter and his family were everywhere.

One beautiful evening, Peter sat by the pool, enjoying the weather. Alex was doing a photoshoot, and the children were with their grandparents.

Peter said to himself, *Life is good.*

One of their maids approached him, saying, "There is an electrician here to see you. He said he has the layout for the next project."

Peter said, "Great—please show him to the library."

When Peter entered the library, he could hardly believe his eyes. He quickly shut the doors, went over to Elwin, and hugged him, saying, "It's great to see you, cousin. How is Tiffany? Sit down—care for a drink?"

Elwin said, "Tiffany is fine. I'm here to tell you about the second phase. By the way, where did you got that gold gun from—the one you have hanging on your wall?"

Peter said, "That's a long story for another day. This room is safe to talk. No one can see into the windows, but we can see out. The room is swept for bugs daily, and the security system is state of the art. Now, what is our next step?"

Elwin replied, "We may want you to run for president. The present membership is destroying their relationship with China, while Russia and North Korea are growing fond of each other. This could become a very serious problem. Our intel shows that 50% of congress members are millionaires with a yearly salary of $174,000. Somethings is wrong there.

"As our spies gather information, we have been sending it to the FBI anonymously. They are investigating 6 senators and 12 congressmen. We believe that with your popularity, you could win the presidency. Especially if we were to hack the voting system as did the present administration did.

"As of now, between Chinese and Latinos we have 25% of the population, and we have 12% of the black population. The rest is white, which accounts for 73%. Your popularity is growing. The polls show that the younger generation would like you to run for president."

Peter said, "And who would be my running mate?"

Elwin replied, "We believe Alicia would be a good candidate. She is a married Latina woman and a college professor."

Peter said, "Has anyone spoken to her about this?"

Elwin said, "Her grandfather and husband are talking to her now."

Peter said, "Let me speak to Alex about it. I'm sure she and Alicia are on the phone already. Also please remember that neither Alicia nor Alex know anything about our plans, and I would like it kept that way."

Elwin said, "I agree."

Peter said, "If father wants to try it this way first, so be it."

Elwin said, "Great! Now that we control 95% of the media and can control the votes in our favor, you have the advantage."

After negotiating with the most powerful members of the Democrat party, Peter and Alicia were put on the ticket as the Democratic presidential nominees. Their platform was excellent, and it reached all of the youth and the older generation without any interference. Between the media influence and the vote hacking, Peter and Alicia were elected as president and vice president.

True to their word, they stopped giving money to foreign countries and instead used tax revenue for their own country. They closed the borders and continued to build the barricade. They opened oil pipelines, got a handle on inflation, and the people were happy. Peter pushed through a bill setting the maximum term limit to eight years for elected government positions. Any officials who opposed this bill were blackmailed by Elwin's team, making them to vote for the bill.

Asian and Latinos were used more and more in movies and advertisements, helping them mix into the American mainstream. The aid money that had once been given to foreign countries was now used for housing for the homeless, free lunches in schools, and other necessities that were once overlooked and underfunded.

Chinese relations with the United States grew stronger by the day. Chinese immigrants entered the country, unknown by the public, and placed in areas with very low populations. They soon had their own police force, and some public schools now taught Chinese. China bought out a lot of US properties and manufacturers.

Everything was going according to plan.

When January came, it was time for the annual presidential speech to all the senators. Members of Congress and presidential staff were waiting for the President to arrive to the session.

President Walker was on Air Force One, heading to Washington for his meeting. He sat at his desk highlighting the achievements he'd accomplished in the first year of his term. His talking points would be closing the border, finishing the pipeline, getting inflation under control, stopping foreign aid and directing that money instead to help Americans.

As Walker reviewed his speech, Wong Way, his personal aid (secretly recommended by Elwin) came up to him and handed him a telegram. Walker read the telegram. Washington, D.C., and the Pentagon had been totally obliviated, and there'd been a cyberattack on all electrical vehicles in the country.

Peter stared at the telegram. *So, it begins*, he thought.

Just then, the pilot's voice came over the speaker saying, "Hold on! Enemy rockets are coming our way!"

Before the enemy rockets could hit, missiles from the president's plane intercepted the enemy's attack, eliminating the threat.

President Walker gave the order to return to Camp David. Once there, he went right to his office where his aids informed him that all members of Congress who had not yet arrived for the planned session had been assassinated.

President Walker told his staff to contact the media and the highest ranking officer for each branch of the military immediately.

I hope my father and cousin know what they are doing.

Sophia Gonzalez, Peter's press secretary (a Mexican-American also recommended by Elwin), entered the office and said to Peter, "Everyone is here."

Peter stood up and thanked her as they both walked to the podium. Peter stood in front of the media with his military staff from each branch of service behind him. Peter started his speech saying, "Citizens of America, we are now under attack from an unknown enemy. The media has informed you of the events that happened to Washington, D.C., and the Pentagon, as well as the assassinations of the congressmen who were not yet in Washington, D.C., at the time of attack. Our intelligence reports that a cyberattack has been made on our nation's electric vehicles, turning them into weapons. Please disconnect them and leave them where they are. As you can see from the video we've released, they launched rockets at Air Force One. Fortunately, we had our own missiles in place to defend ourselves. Our country is in chaos, but it stops today."

He continued, "As of now, our military is on high alert. Our country is now under martial law. I am asking everybody to obey the law, your governors will be your new leaders and point of contact. I will be having a video meeting with them later, but for now, these are the new laws.

1. I'm asking all governors to activate the national guard, which will work closely with the police Department,

2. All borders will be closed. Anybody trying to get in will be shot. Already, a number of terrorists have been found trying to cross the border and have been neutralized.

3. Any rioters will be considered a terrorist and dealt with accordingly.

4. I urge all citizens to keep their weapons and use them in defense of your property. Try to record any instances of self-defense to show authorities—this way you will not be charged. I suggest all big stores use taser guns and hire your own security.

5. For the security of all, transgenders are no longer recognized. There are only two genders—male and female—and whichever one you were born as is what you are. The rest are a wide range of mental disorders, should you believe you are not what you were born, and you tried to force it on other people, you will be arrested and put in jail. This is for your own protection and the citizens of America, because the enemy will use it against us.

6. Any lawyers who protest these laws will be disbarred.

Make no mistake—we are under attack. And we must stick to-gether. As hard as the above laws are, if we obey these laws, we will survive."

After everyone left, Peter sat in his chair, thinking about his friend, Vice President Alicia and her husband Manuel, saddened that they were casualties of the attack.

Alex rushed into the office, crying and yelling, "Is it true? Is it true?"

Peter stood up, took her in his arms, and said, "Yes, it is true."

Alex looked up at Peter with tears in her eyes and said, "Why?"

Peter replied, "I don't know. We will find out."

A few hours later, Peter sat at his desk as little by little each gover-nor joined the video conference.

When they'd all logged in, Peter addressed the governors, looking carefully into each face. To faces of shock and disbelief, Peter in-formed them that from that moment on, they would be the leaders of their state, would be paid $200,000.00 annually, and would be expected to support all decisions he made.

"From now on, all persons arrested will go before a judge and have bail set for that crime. Should the judge refuse, remove the judge."

Peter knew which governors would protest, and he had replace-ments ready for them. As he expected, the New York and Califor-nia governors objected.

Peter replied, "I'm sorry you feel that way. New York governor, you are being replaced with fleet Admiral Anthony Montalbano, who will work closely with the lieutenant governor."

The New York governor's office doors opened and two military policemen walked in and asked the New York governor to go with them. The New York government started to scream, "How dare you? You can't do this!"

One policeman said, "The president said I can, so I will. You will also be locked up for embezzling over $1 million of city funds."

The military police took him out and the fleet admiral took his seat.

The California governor looked at Peter, saying, "Don't you dare…"

The governor's doors opened, and two military police came in, asking him to come with them. When he refused, they forcefully took him out of the room.

"You are arrested for taking bribes from the cartel and other companies for your own personal interest," Peter said as they took him away. "As for the rest of you," he said to the governors, "should you not want to be a team player, please say so now."

Everyone was quiet.

"Good. General Tim Scott will be taking the California governor's place, and he will work closely with the lieutenant governor. General David Odenmatt of the Marines will be ready to assist all those who need help enforcing the new laws in their states. Many you may not like what's happening, but for the good of the country, this must be done.

"Now, going forward, we must not have large crowds anywhere. Try to keep your citizens informed. I will inform you of any updates as they come in. In the meantime, the generals are the new governors of the California and New York states. This meeting is now adjourned."

The following months were crucial to get control of the country. Throughout the nation, there was chaos. The gays held a rally, and unfortunately for them, bombs were thrown into their rally, killing at least half of them. College students protested too, and bombs were placed in the schools killing many. The papers blamed Hamas and other unknown terrorists. Amid the chaos, looters ran rampant, but the stores were ready with their security. It didn't take long until looting ended after seeing other looters being shot with tasers then arrested.

Rioters destroyed property, and hurt innocent people. The rioters were met with police and military force. Many of the rioters were shot, and those who weren't were arrested and put into jail with no hearing.

Around June, things started to calm down. Most of the country was happy that law and order had returned.

Months later, as Peter sat in front of the governors, he watched their faces carefully. Most of them were afraid for their own position and were willing to do whatever Peter suggested to keep their position. The generals looked like they had their hands full, but they had their armies and police to back them. The first one to speak was Fleet Admiral Montalban.

"Millions of dollars have been lost through scams, like covering license plates when going through tolls. At least $1 billion a year has been lost."

Peter replied, "Do what you must. You're in charge of that state now. Be careful, though. The enemy is still out there."

General Scott stated that California was in complete chaos. "Even with military enforcement, it's very difficult to control all the crime."

Peter replied, "Do what is necessary to protect our citizens."

Just then, Way entered the room, handing Peter a sealed envelope.

Peter opened it and read it silently. When finished, he put the letter back in the envelope and sat quiet for a few moments. He then addressed the governors and generals.

"The following has been brought to my attention by the FBI. Evidently, the former governor of California made a deal with the Chinese president allowing 21,000 Chinese immigrants into California for a half billion dollars. They are in our country now. Presently, they pose no threat, and compared to the other immigrants allowed in by the previous administration, they are few."

Most of the governors showed no concern and wanted to know why there was no media coverage of the riots and some other issues they felt their citizens should know.

Peter replied, "It is the media's responsibility to protect the people from propaganda and to let the people know the truth. The media does not does write in favor of the gay rally or riots but informs of what actually happened at the riots. They write about the destroyed businesses, the innocent people killed and injured. Before, the news was not telling the truth, everybody pitied the poor rioters being arrested, not talking about the destroyed property and how a lot of small mom and pop businesses were closed down due to these rioters. So why should the news write in favor of them? The news now tells the truth. That's the way it should be. My question to you is: who do you serve?"

The governors got the message.

Peter replied, "Good. Now, I would like you all to set up voting booths so our citizens can vote on some new laws I am proposing.

1. All pedophiles will be chemically castrated. Should a pedophile injure or kill a child, they will be immediately executed.

2. All convicts on death row will be immediately executed by hanging.

3. Every high school will have mandatory classes called "Life". Students will learn sewing, car maintenance, taxes, basic first aid, basic cooking, woodworking, social etiquette, personal finance, and cursive.

4. All schools will have armed security guards and free lunch programs, paid for by the government.

5. Parents will be allowed to spank their children with the stipulations that they spank only their own children, only on the buttocks, and only with their open palm.

7. Because of the cyber-attacks, we will no longer support electric vehicles. We will now focus on hydrogen energy. It's much cheaper and cleaner.

8. All public schools will say the Pledge of Allegiance every morning.

9. Do you want the Congress positions back?

10. Do you want to vote on important laws?

Please contact your local news channels and explain the laws on the ballots . Communicate that we expect every eligible citizen to vote.

Unfortunately, due to the corruption of the former administration, only in-person voting will be allowed."

Peter finished, "Law and order *will* be restored."

HOLIDAYS

Around Hanukkah and Christmas, there was a lot of unrest with the Palestinians. They were railing against Israel, Christians, and the United States. Peter knew something had to be done.

Peter spoke to the governors and said, "I believe that Hamas is behind the terror cells. The Palestinians have held numerous illegal rallies and there were no threats or bombings at their events, unlike the others. This makes me believe that many of them are in the terror cells. For the security of our country, I have negotiated an agreement with Brazil and South Africa for the American-based Palestinians to be relocated to these countries. Air Force General Douglas Hassle will be in charge of this project. They are being rounded up as we speak. They will be loaded on air buses and flown to Brazil and South Africa. Once there they will be moved to a designated area as dictated by the Brazilian and South African governments. It should take 15 – 20 air buses, and hopefully that will lessen the threat to our country.

"Next on the agenda is the Chinese immigration organized by the former California governor. The leader of China has informed me that the previous California governor was paid half a billion dollars to allow Chinese military vessels to refuel off our coastline. Men had already been put in place to build the berthing docks for the vessels. For now, that is not going to happen.

"But I explained that we would like to take advantage of China's advanced engineering technology to build affordable modular homes. If they would assist in building these homes throughout our country for the homeless and those less able to afford housing, we would pay their engineers $5,000.00 per home.

"They, of course, accepted."

MEDIA NEWS

Peter stood in front of the media and addressed the citizens of America.

"Good evening, my fellow Americans. I promised to give you an update on the Palestinian crisis and the Chinese immigration crisis.

"As of now, the Palestinians have been relocated to Brazil and South Africa. I have made an agreement with the Chinese government to build modular homes for our homeless citizens, in order to put the immigrants to work, improving our nation. Each home will cost less than $5,000. We will have teams using half of the Chinese construction personnel that the previous governor of California let in and half of our own construction personnel, which will help our unemployment go down. It should take less than one day to do 10 homes, so we should be moving along rapidly.

"I have also asked these impressive Chinese engineers to help us find clean water solutions in Flint, Michigan, and they were more than willing to help us. This will put even more of our unemployed and the remaining Chinese immigrants to work.

"January 10 is a big day for our country. We will vote for the future of our nation. I am asking everyone to vote and, if you agree, to pass these laws, not only to help lower lawlessness, but to help improve our standard of living.

JANUARY 10

Peter sat in his office waiting for the voting results. Way Wong, Peter's personal aid, entered and whispered that Elwin didn't have to do anything to manipulate the votes. His laws had all passed by a landslide.

When the polls had closed, Peter requested a video conference with all the governors.

Once all the governors were online, Peter addressed them, "Now that you are the sole representatives of your state, and Congress is obsolete, it is your responsibility to make sure these laws are put in place and obeyed.

"I would like each of you to appoint a representative to liaise with the Chinese to bring your state the help it needs. Each of these representatives will be a part of a new department called United, which will be a joint effort between the Chinese aide officials and your state liaisons. "

Nods of approval rippled on his screen. Everything was going as planned.

"Until our next meeting, then. Please put what you want to talk about on the next agenda. Until then, God bless America."

ONE YEAR LATER

———————

A little over a year later, Peter held a ceremony at the locations of the attacks on America. Members of every media outlet were there, courtesy of Elwin. Peter's speech was touching, inflaming pride in American people. The areas that were once Washington, D.C., and the Pentagon were now beautiful parks and lakes with monuments memorializing the victims.

After the ceremony, Peter sat in his office wondering what to do about the recent wave of antisemitism facing the country. He knew that it started with the Jews, but next would be the Christians, followed by the Chinese, and any other religion or race that got in the way of Hamas. He had watched it all throughout history, so he came up with an idea. He would restart the draft. Anyone aged 18 through 28 would be enlisted.

He spoke to his aid, who told Elwin's contact about Peter's plan. The next day, the media started saying that North Korea, the Arab nations, and Russia had formed an alliance, creating the most powerful joint military force in the world.

After weeks of the media telling how dangerous is for America to be left with only South Korea and Japan as allies, Peter held a press conference to inform the American people that the draft would be reinstated.

The plan for the draft was approved by all the governors.

Peter said that anyone of draftable age could avoid the draft by leaving the country, but they could never return as a citizen.

It went better than Peter had expected.

10% of those drafted left the country, including immigrants, never to return. This gave the governors the green light to shut down many colleges that were troublesome, all on the pretense that the colleges were no longer profitable with so few students.

It was time to contact Elwin.

THE POWER OF THE MEDIA

Peter watched the media and was amazed at how his cousin manipulated the public into accepting the influx of Chinese and Spanish immigrants. The two races were in all the commercials, movies, and shows. Their food dominated the culinary industry. Their languages were taught in public schools. Elwin kept up the story of Hamas' persecution, while keeping the idea of having China merge with the US for protection against Russia, North Korea, and the Arab Empire.

A few weeks later, the media reported that about half of those incarcerated in the United States had been killed by a strange virus. The FBI looked into it and found evidence that it was chemical warfare by the Hamas because those prisons catered to gays.

Peter sat at his desk daring not to ask how his cousin had pulled that off when Way came in and whispered in Peter's ear. "Your cousin said, 'You're welcome.'"

He sat in amazement, stunned that his cousin had such an exquisite underground network of spies.

The next day, Peter sent out word that he would like to have a video conference with all the governors at 1 PM.

When all the governors had logged on, Peter began.

"I'm sure you would all like to know what we're going to do about the education system's failings of late. My plan is to have the citizens vote on whether to allow in educators to come in from other countries and help bring our system up to the standards of the world.

"We also need to be aware that our population is growing fast with diversity of races. Presently the Chinese and the Latinos are the fastest growing population in our country. We should all keep this in mind when leading our states and be considerate of them.

"I'd also like to put on the ballot our request for China to become part of our country. We can learn much from one another. As I'm sure everyone has seen, when Russia, North Korea, and the Arab nations put their fleets in the Atlantic Ocean, outnumbering us, China's joined our own and we outnumbered the enemy fleet. This shows their commitment to be a part of our nation.

"And this isn't the first time they've helped us, either. During the first world war, the Chinese sent over 2 million workers to Europe to help us fight, over 1 million of them died. During World War II, they refused to sell raw materials to Japan, who then invaded and killed 35 million Chinese. Imagine the strength we'd gain together in the future. Please remember this. It is time to vote."

Peter closed his laptop and called for his press secretary. "Call a press conference. I need to address the nation."

The arrangements were made for the vote, and before the polls opened, President Walker stood in the front of the podium and addressed the citizens of America. "The decision we make today is of great importance. Will we allow China to merge with America, joining our two great nations? Before we vote, please let me tell you a few of the facts.

"China has been our ally since World War II. Despite the US deficit, cross-border trade with China contributes numerous benefits including more jobs for each country, lower-cost goods, and a higher standard of living. Cooperation between China and United States will create a huge demand in the world market. In 14 more years, our population will evolve. We will soon be 50% Chinese and Latino, 12% African-Americans, and 32%, white.

"And how our military is diminishing. If the United States were to be plunged into war, we might be able to hold our own at first, but should it be a lengthy conflict, the United States would be in trouble. 80% of those within draft age cannot pass the physical exam. What's more, even fewer are willing to join the military. At present, the average age of a military person is 28—to replace that person, it's getting harder and harder.

"North Korea and Russia are joining forces. North Korea has the world's largest navy fleet. Russia has a massive military force. They are readying their people for war. War against us.

"If we were to merge with China, it would benefit both countries economically and militarily. We would fly two flags together, and we would work together with a special committee on both sides to iron out any problems that might arise. Together, we could be a stronger nation. I leave it up to you, the citizens of the United States of America."

On June 19, 1966, I was to be married. Instead I was pledging my life to our country and becoming a member of the United States Army. I was sent to Fort Gordon in Georgia where I was trained to be a soldier. It turned out that I was an expert sharpshooter. Right before finishing basic training, I was told I was going to being trained as a sniper, but for whatever reason half my outfit came down with pneumonia. I believe it was the five-mile hike we did in the pouring rain. Once out of the hospital, I could not continue my training, so I was sent to Fort Story to train on boats. I really did not know what the program was, but as we all know, we have no choice.

Long story short, I was trained to drive various vessels. Not too bad. I and my friend, another expert rifleman, graduated at the top of our class. My friend Dave and I received orders for Germany. While we were congratulating ourselves, the sergeant came over and crossed out 'Germany' and put 'Vietnam', while saying that, where I was going, he only wanted the best.

We were to report to Fort Dix in three days. I told the Sarge that I had not seen my girlfriend since I had entered the Army. He replied, "If she loves you, she will wait."

I did get to see her on my way for a few hours, but they felt like minutes. We landed up in Long Bin. That night we had incoming mail. It was addressed to whoever was in camp. It did not care if you were a cook or clerk. Whoever received the mail cashed in their check. The Sarge saw our medals on our dress uniforms, handed us a rifle, and we went into the bush looking for them. We did not find them.

The next day, Dave and I were standing in Cam Rahn Bay, and Sarge was happy to see us. He gave us our assignments. We had the privilege of carrying five tons of explosives from ship to shore. I carried to the 5th division Green Berets. For safety reasons, I never carried a gun, but I did have support from the air. When I came in after a long day, the cooks always put something aside for us, and the clerk always had our paperwork ready.

After 11 months, 29 days, and the loss of many boats, I went home without firing a shot.

To me anyone who is or was in the military is a veteran.

If you want to know more, read my book, *A Gang Members Tale*.

Thank you,
Wolfie

Print ISBN 978-1-62023-806-6

Veteran Crisis Line

800-273-8255